This book belongs to:

David Walliams

PRESENTS...

For Indigo. Welcome to the world.
With love, David x

For Gwilym.
With love, Adam x

First published in hardback in the United Kingdom by HarperCollins *Children's Books* in 2022

HarperCollins *Children's Books* is a division of HarperCollins*Publishers* Ltd
1 London Bridge Street, London SE1 9GF

www.harpercollins.co.uk

HarperCollins*Publishers*,
Macken House, 39/40 Mayor Street Upper, Dublin 1, D01 C9W8, Ireland

1 3 5 7 9 10 8 6 4 2

Text copyright © David Walliams 2022
Illustrations copyright © Adam Stower 2022
Cover lettering of author's name copyright © Quentin Blake 2010

ISBN: 978-0-00-830576-5

Printed in Italy

GRANNYSAURUS

ILLUSTRATED
BY THE AMAZING
Adam Stower

HarperCollins *Children's Books*

Do YOU love to stay up late?

This is a story about a boy who NEVER wanted to go to bed, especially when he was having a sleepover at his granny's house.

"Bedtime!" announced Granny, as she and her grandson finished their dinosaur jigsaw together.

"But Mum and Dad let me stay up until way past midnight!" fibbed the boy.

"Ha! Ha! I'm not falling for that old one, Spike! It's bedtime!"

"NOT FAIR!" he said. "How come **you** are allowed to stay up **late**?"

"Because I'm much, MUCH **older** than **you**!"

"I bet you are as **old** as this **dinosaur**, Granny!" said Spike cheekily, pointing to the puzzle.

Spike *sprinted* up the stairs,

dived

into

his

pyjamas,

and leaped into bed.

"Granny**SAURUS** is *STARVING*! Are any juicy little ones still wide awake?" came a voice in the dark. "**GRRR!**"

The boy shut his eyes and pretended to snore.

"ZZZZ! ZZZZ!"

Then Spike opened one eye and . . .

... spied the shadow of a DINOSAUR!

He yanked the covers over his head
and tried to sleep.
However . . .

He woke up to find his bedroom BOOMING!

DOOF! DOOF!

DOOF!

The whole house was pulsating with music and FLASHING lights.

So, he tiptoed down the stairs . . .

and opened the living-room door . . .

Granny was having a **party** and Spike was NOT invited . . .

It was a DINO DISCO!

Grannysaurus was behind the decks,

spinning some bangin' tunes!

Well, she *was* a SPIN-OSAURUS!

Dinosaurs were MOVING!

Dinosaurs were GROOVING!

Still in his pyjamas Spike joined the party!
He boogied with a BRONTOSAURUS!

He strutted his stuff with
a STEGOSAURUS!

And he got on down with a GIGANOTOSAURUS!

When Grannysaurus spotted her grandson out of bed, she STOPPED the music.

SCRATCH!

"OOH!" moaned the disappointed dinosaurs.

"SPIKE! Go back to bed!" ordered Grannysaurus.

"NO!" replied Spike, crossing his arms. "I'm going to stay up all night and BOOGIE!"

"This is a DINOS-ONLY disco!" she replied. "BEDTIME!"

"You'll have to CATCH ME first!" said Spike.

With that, he *RACED* out of the living room to find a **hiding place**.

In the downstairs loo, there was a tetchy TRICERATOPS perusing a paper.

"DO YOU MIND!"

On Granny's bed, there was a couple of BRACHIOSAURUSES bouncing up and down.

BOING!

BOING!

"BUZZ OFF!"

And **splashing** about in the bath was a huge PLESIOSAURUS.

SpLISH!

SPLASH!

SpLOSH!

"HOW DARE YOU!"

So, Spike *RACED* back to the living room . . .

"BEDTIME!"

shouted ALL the dinosaurs.

"NEVER!" replied Spike.
Though he was feeling more than a *little* tired.

"Then just you wait until REX arrives!"
warned Grannysaurus.

"REX? You don't mean . . . ?"

Grannysaurus nodded and grinned.

BOOF!

BOOF!

BOOF!

The whole house
began to
SHAKE.

RATTLE!

Spike looked out of the **window** to see a **huge**

TYRANNOSAURUS REX

lumbering down the road.

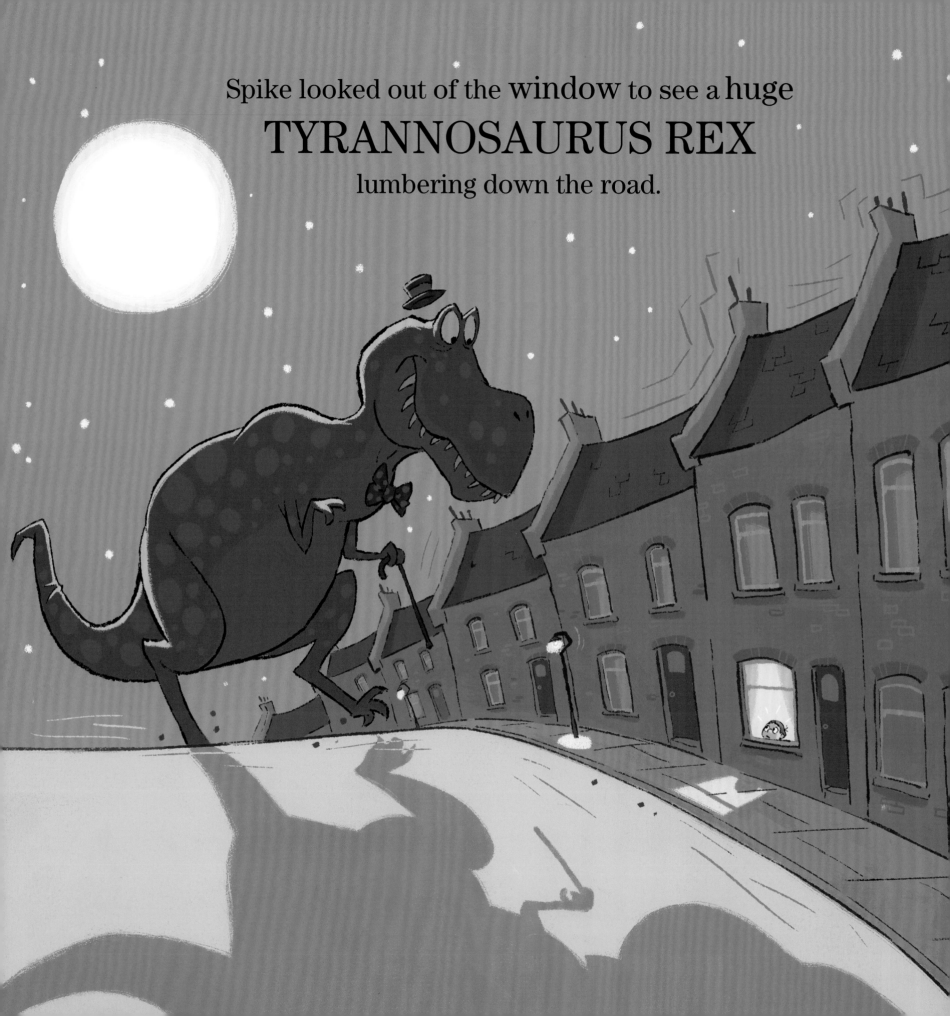

Being a **T-REX**, he was far **too big** to fit through the front door.
Instead, Rex *BURST* through the **wall**.

SMASH!

Half the house fell in as dust exploded everywhere.

KABOOM!

But Spike was too *QUICK.*
He charged up
the stairs . . .

before leaping onto Rex's head.
"You CAN'T catch me now!"
he exclaimed.

When Grannysaurus
STOMPED
up the **stairs** to
GRAB him . . .

Spike *SURFED* down
the dinosaur's back.

"WOOHOO!"

"SEND HIM TO BED, REX!" called out Grannysaurus.

"Right you are!"

When Spike reached the end of the dinosaur's **tail**, Rex *FLICKED* it.

WHIP!

The boy was shot into the **air**.

"*ARGH!*"

Spike soared HIGH UP . . .

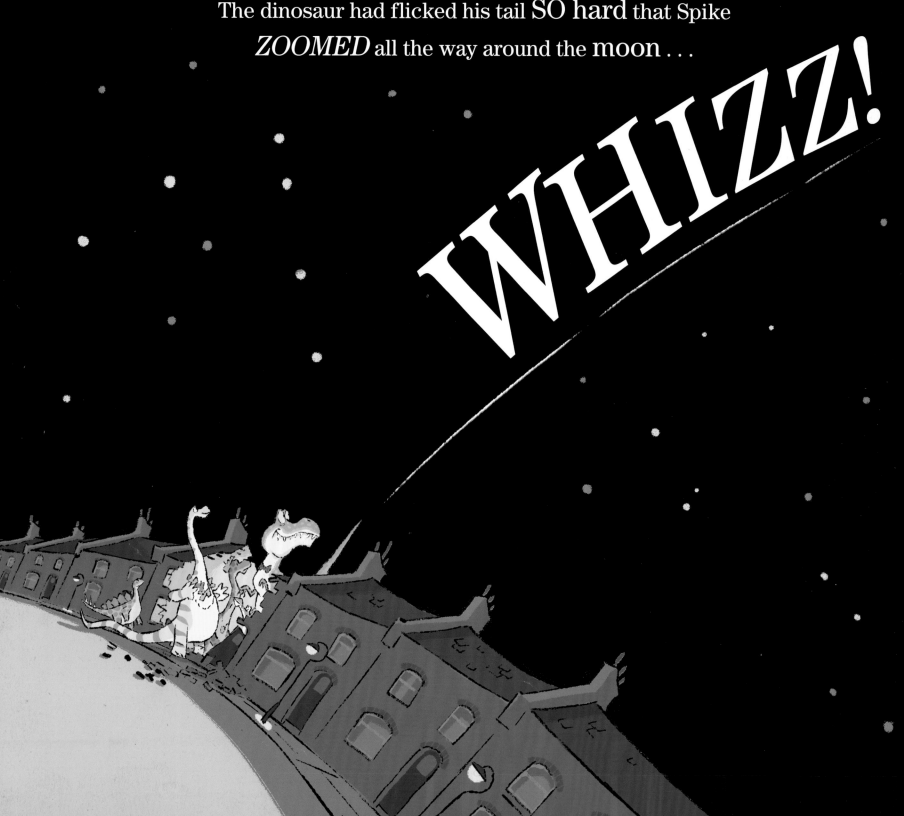

. . . into the NIGHT sky.

"OOPS!" muttered the T-Rex as they all watched him go.
The dinosaur had flicked his tail SO hard that Spike
ZOOMED all the way around the moon . . .

WHIZZ!

. . . before

tumbling

back

to

Earth.

"NOOO!"

By a stroke of **enormous** good fortune, the boy **crash-landed** straight back onto his **own** bed!

THUMP!

"OOF!"

"NOW GO TO SLEEP!"

called up all the dinosaurs.

Not fancying another lap around the **moon**, Spike yanked the **covers** over his head, and **shut his eyes** tight. In a moment he was in a deep, deep sleep.

"ZZZZ! ZZZz!"

From that day on, Spike went to bed ridiculously early . . .

He was determined to be **fast asleep** *before* the **dinosaurs** came out to **play** for the night.

As should YOU . . .

So come on now, bedtime!